Behind a Wardrobe in Atlantis

First Published in the UK in 2014 by Mantle Arts

ISBN 978-0-951504062

Mantle Lane Press
Springboard Centre
Mantle Lane
Coalville
LE67 3DW
www.mantlelanepress.co.uk
www.mantlearts.org.uk

Printed and bound in the UK by
Imprint Digital, Upton Pyne, Exeter, EX5 5HY

Cover illustration by Sam Pash
www.sampashillustration.com

Behind a Wardrobe in Atlantis

Emma J. Lannie

For my sister Lindsey

Contents

Behind A Wardrobe In Atlantis

I've been practising holding my breath. All my life, really, one way or another. But especially now, especially for this.

I'm knee-deep, my toes sliding in the silt. My shoes are on the shore, piled up with my clothes. There are a hundred ways to erase a life.

This is something we would have done together. On long nights, when the clanking of radiators keeps me awake, I think of that tiny point in time and it still makes my heart catch, it still kicks my feet from underneath me.

This day has yet to begin. The sun is caught, stuck, and the other stars have just left holes, a million tiny goodbyes. Still, in the space between yesterday and today, a slow light bleeds through. It makes me silver like a fish, and as I wade deeper, the water circles my thighs, swallows me like one of its own.

I've made it to the middle a hundred times. In the

there-and-back of it, my body has learned quickness, my arms know the exact shapes to be. Today, I don't even break the surface of the water. As though everything has been leading up to this.

It was more than scratching a biro into door-frames, more than him being three inches taller than me. There were things that we did. Things in the dark, things that mattered at the time. Like sleeping back to back, fusing our skin inch by inch, chasing the warm. Like trying to guess what the other was doing, what shapes were being made. An arm stretched out to the side, or a foot raised and waggled; a hand becoming a bird, a deer, a spider.

Last time, I found my old window, the glass still intact. The house, without sunlight, had lost its squareness, had become a smoother, browner version of itself. The ground floor windows were gone, as though my mother had left them open, inviting the river into our home. For years afterwards I dreamed of black torrents splintering doors.

I take a breath. My body knows the rest. It dives down to the places it knew well. The yard where I learned to ride a bike, Mum running behind with her hand on the saddle, steadying me before letting me go. Pavements I grazed my knees on, and the wide steps where I sat each July making rose-petal perfume in old milk bottles. All these places are

8

part of me, mixed in with the blood and lymph, sleeping in the chambers of my heart. The way into the house is through my window. I rest my forehead on the glass, leave an imprint of an older self there. My fingers heave at the wood until it gives and I swim through the gap.

I used to bring him gifts. I filled jars with breezes, trapped caterpillars in ice-cream tubs. I gave him flat stones and newts and sycamore seeds. And in return, he'd give me words. He wrote them on whatever was to hand. I'd wake to find he'd conjured me into stories in the curtains, find more chapters inside cereal boxes, woven into the snap crackle pop of everyday. The myth of me found its way into pinafore pockets, and underneath carpets, and onto the inside of lampshades.

There's still a bulb hanging from the fitting. All those wires, all those connections, all shut off in just one day. I flick the switch, hoping somehow this one light got missed, but it didn't, and the moss from it sticks furry, green, to my finger.

I hadn't seen him in a long time. My life took me out of the spaces we'd shared, flung me far from the new place we grew to call home. But even from the bottom of a lake, there is a certain pull exerted by memory. Things we remember in our muscles and bones. Dancing around the room, my feet on his, while Brian Wilson sang God Only Knows through the tinny speakers of my hand-me-down stereo. Him climbing the laburnum tree and shaking the branches, while I twirled underneath, catching the petals in cupped hands, pretending they were gold. Then Mum screaming about poison, slapping them out of my grasp, pulling on his foot to get him to come down.

We left the things we didn't need. Things we had outgrown. The wicker chair at the top of the stairs. His chest of drawers with the bottoms falling out. My wardrobe. Moth-ball scented and heavy as a lorry. We happily left my wardrobe behind while our house waited for the lake to come. The wardrobe is the only thing in the room now, apart from me and a few fish. It seems even bigger than it was, the wood, wet, has swollen, has made it a giant.

I've been reading him the stories, trying to fill in his gaps. There are some things that are never erased: I will always be his sister. I've been piecing together the words, gathering scraps of old cardboard and cloth, paper and metal. But there's a part of it missing. I don't know how it ends.

The water helps me move the wardrobe just far enough out so I can get behind it. I see the words straight away, written in red wax three inches tall. They are our difference in height. They are the only distance between us. I pull gently at the wallpaper and it comes away from the wall. I carry it with me all the way to the surface.

By the time I get to his bedside, the paper has crumbled away. But it doesn't matter; I remember every word. And it's a really good ending.

Rapunzelled

From inside the tower, the world feels different. It's a reminder of the roundness of things, how everything happens in circles, how nothing ever ends.

My sister is eating boiled sweets. She drops the wrappers on the floor. In the half-light, I hear the cellophane scrunch just before she lets go. We are not spending the day here. She has more on her itinerary. She clicks her camera and tells me to stand very still. She wants to let as much light into the camera as possible. This takes time in these dimly-lit places. Not so much when we're out on the cliffs or by the sea, like we were an hour ago. She had me put my feet in rock pools while she freeze-framed anemones in black and white. Afterwards, we sat and picked at immoveable limpets, wishing for a different kind of strength.

We are the same in height and build and how we look. I am older than her by a few years, but she is the one who has things to do, and so when she asks, I comply. She governs my life in such ways. She is the only structure I really have.

This tower was built as a defence during the war. Towers like this one line the coast, mostly abandoned now. I would live in one, if I could. Something about the roundness makes me feel safe. The heavy walls encircling me. I find a certain comfort in this kind of claustrophobia.

My sister takes the picture, finally. I twist my neck from side to side, shrug the stiffness out. She makes a reality in which I am here always, my feet in the soft dust, my hair tied back in a braid.

She asks me to move to the wall, directs me in my mannerisms, tilts my head against it until my forehead presses into the stone. I do this with trees sometimes. I try to listen for the creak of growing. But this is more like being inside of the tree, pushed up against the trunk, with me the one trying to grow, even though I know I'm dying.

The only sound in here is our breathing and the soft whir of the camera, the infrequent click of the shutter. If I were to move, I would make myself a ghost in these photographs. The lines of me would blur. I would become transparent. My sister and I have experimented with this in the past, her urging me to run across rooms and back again. Every so often she would catch the wildness in my eyes as I ran. Through her pictures I become aware of myself, of how I am and how I can be. But these new pictures are heavy, tied down with process. My sister needs me to be still, un-moveable. She wants to capture me.

She wants to capture me.

And so I let her.

Bee

Ow. The sting is a shock. The bee drops to the windowsill. I examine the heel of my palm where the stinger is still attached. The image of my hand spread against the net curtains, and the bee, will stay with my small daughter for all of her life.

There is so much sadness in this room. The bee lies dead on the windowsill. My hand throbs. It is a wonder to me that I can feel anything. My husband is somewhere else. There are other rooms to be emptied, closed down. He is in one of them, and I hope that he has found the space to cry, to own his sadness.

This is just a house now. The room where my daughter played shop, with tins emptied from cupboards, is just a room. My husband's mother will never again swap pennies for tins of mandarin segments. I will be the one to play this game with my daughter from now on, but my efforts will be hurried and brief, bookended by feeds and changing nappies and trying to figure out what I am doing with my life.

My husband's mother loved me like a daughter. When she came to stay, it was underwritten with the idea that she would come back here, when she was better.

The stinger is not lodged deep. I scrape it out with my fingernail. There is baking soda in the kitchen cupboard still, and I make a paste with water and apply it to the sting. My daughter clings to my legs, her arms wrapped tight around my thighs. I reassure her I am okay.

This is difficult to do with her here. My husband wanted to leave her at my sister's, with the baby, but yesterday she called me a liar. When we got here this morning, she knocked on the door while my husband struggled with the key. I don't know what rules govern the dead, but knocking before you enter their home is a good politeness, I think. Something I would also have done, had I been here alone. Once the door was open, she darted inside, shouting, "Nana" into every room. My husband stalled at the door. I went in, my heart in pieces.

All rooms exhausted, my daughter came to me slow, defeated. This was the only place she thought her Nana could be. I lifted her. She wrapped her limbs tight around me.

I know you're supposed to keep these things from children. But my daughter is four years old and wiser than the lot of us.

We go back into the front room. She rests her chin on the windowsill and whispers to the bee. I don't hear what she says. I take the nets down and my daughter helps me fold them, our arms wide, our hands coming together in a dance that is all about the lives of women. A dance that is also a kind of prayer.

Minotaur

We live on this island and it is all right. I have a secret brother I'm not supposed to know about. I spend my nights curled up in his bed, and we tell each other stories and he teaches me what it's like to be older.

Only my mum visits him. My dad is not his dad, and that's part of what the big secret is, but there's more to it than that. People tell their own stories. My brother is a hundred things and more. But to me, he is only my brother. The one who taught me to trust my body. The one who showed me what the world could be.

We live on this island and it's all right, but because of my brother, I know there is another world out there, a place un-mapped and wild. It sounds like a place I would like. A place I could inhabit with my brother, and we could wander the open spaces and be free, be together.

My brother wears his bad reputation on his head, bold. He is a gnashing of teeth and a slamming against walls.

He often comes to bed with blood on his hands. But once it's dried it doesn't stain anymore. I pick the clots from his skin as he breathes lullabies into my hair. In his bed, cradled against the fur of him, I am completely safe. I am where I was always meant to be.

And when he wakes in the night from bad dreams, then it's my turn to soothe him. I hold his head in my arms, stroke the terror away. The scent of us changes then, and a soft calm settles on us. His breath settles on me, in all the places it can find, and my hands do the things older hands do, and morning sometimes comes before we know it.

We live on this island and it is all right. Because it won't be for too much longer now. People say my brother is an animal. And that's true, but only I know to what delicious extent. They only have their own ideas, based on what they don't know. But I know the gleam in his eye and the weight of him, things they will never know. People say he has horns, but that can mean something else entirely. They say he is a monster, and I can understand why, but again, I have my own interpretations of that, and it doesn't change the fact that I love him.

Nobody knows we spend this time here. No body knows the ways in which he has shaped me. His mouth, with his words, and other things. And his hands, hands that could crush a skull, on me they slide gentle, leaving goose bumps in their wake. He came before me, he is older, but he shares that with me, lets me know something of how that feels. He teaches me. There is talk of being lost, but I have never been that. I know the paths to take through this labyrinth. I have always found my way home.

Not Gretel

This is a different kind of breadcrumb trail. More permanent, if not completely. I am not yet sure I will need it to help me find my way back. It's still bright out. Here, where the trees are less dense, the sunlight filters down and is golden. Even though this forest will get darker the deeper I go, there will still be daylight for some hours yet. The day will exist outside of this forest, and a girl will push her brother as he leaves the house too slowly, a husband will kiss his wife goodbye. In a garden with a single tree, a dog will spring to its feet, ears alert, and then settle again, circling its small patch of grass before letting its muzzle sink down into the tiny fronds. There will be birds migrating South for winter, setting off too early, tricked by seasons out of kilter.

But I will be in the forest, spinning this woollen thread behind me, not quite Ariadne. I'm not betraying anyone. And not Gretel either. There is no exile or entrapment.

Where I'm headed, the forest floor barely sees sunlight. There is only leaf-mulch, broken down by earthworms and ants and small purposeful things. There is the crack of twigs beneath my feet. I am the largest animal that comes into these woods.

I am lost. I have the woollen line to lead me out, but it's not that kind of lost. It's the loss of not-belonging, of no-one knowing what time I climbed out of bed, or what I ate for breakfast, or how my face looked as I stepped out into the day. Lost in the way that unwanted things are. Discarded. Forgotten.

There's an Inuit custom of walking anger out, walking as far as the anger still exists. Then marking the place the anger ends with a stick. Measuring the distance of the anger. This is a different thing. I'm walking a line but the thing I'm walking off is not anger, I am walking off a sadness. I am not sure if there will be an end to it.

The trees grow much closer together now. Saplings from the parent trees must have grown here when there was a lot more room, a lot less canopy. And now I can't pass one tree without brushing against another. I let my hands rest on the bark as I move through, from one tree to another. There is a stillness here that I've never found anywhere else. It lets me slow my breathing right down, slow my frantic heartbeat, until I don't even remember who I am or what I was worried or upset about all this time. It's just me and these trees. The branches and leaves and trunks, the moss and the bark and ivy, sometimes, or fungi in all their myriad shapes and colours. My wool is red. The line is red. The line I will gather up, or choose not to. It might stay unravelled in this forest for a while yet. Or longer than that. The line is a courtesy, and a safety net, and a last request: someone find me. I have pills. If I do this, I choose to fall asleep. I have always felt safest in the woods. I tell myself maybe I can move somewhere with lots of trees, maybe I can find a wood of my own to live in. But I can't tell if I'm just trying to cling on to something through fear, or whether I really do have a spark of hope left in me.

I go through my day to day without speaking to another soul. I sit at a desk in front of a screen and I type numbers and words and commands into the ether. Execute. Execute. Execute. No one knows or cares who I am, just that I fulfil my obligations, complete the tasks I've been assigned. I am invisible. I may not even exist.

There are days when I forget the sound of my own voice.

I stop to rest my legs. The trees are older here. Their

bark cracked and full of life. My eyes are used to the low light now. Outside, in the world, the sun will be high, casting short shadows. There will be traffic and noise and radios, music hanging in the air, pulsing and bouncing and resonating across rooms and driveways and fields. It is not silent here, in the forest. There is activity everywhere. It's just that none of it is human.

And then I see her. A flash of pink. At first I think it's a bird, but as she comes into view, I realise it's a woman. She has on a bright pink cardigan. Strung out behind her is a yellow thread, the mass of which she holds in her hands like an offering. She could be my mirror, in a different colour scheme.

We each remain where we are, stopped, aware of one another but uncertain what to do. She sees me. I see her. In the half light of this deep dark forest, we have been seen, noticed. We are visible. We are not alone.

Across the distance we raise our arms in the silent gesture of hello. She stares into me for a long time. Opening myself, I stare back.

Noah's Daughter

The face she has is not entirely her own. It is a
composite of the face of her mother and the face of her
father. Most people are only interested in the features
that mirror her father's. He has been dead for most of
her life, but people still seek her out, and stare, even ask
sometimes if they can touch her face for a split second.
She doesn't always say no. Something in the way these
boys ask, quietly, mumbling, lets her see a little of how her
father was, allows her to feel him up close again, calloused
fingers gentle against her skin.

She feels undeserving of this reverence. She accepts
it humbly. Behind the face of her father she is a person
of her own. She has faults. She gets angry because she
remembers less of him than everyone else. They possess
her father in a way she never can. All she has of him

is a face the shape of a heart, and eyes the colour of cornflowers left out in the sun too long. When she listens to his friends talking about him and the things they used to do together, she becomes nostalgic for something she's never had, grieves the space his death has left in her life.

With girls, it's simple. She's just one of them. Her face is a canvas to be slicked with the colours of the day. With girls, she feels her father's ghost dissipate as her body takes over. She is breasts and pale skin. Her muscles hold her bones steady as she climbs inside dresses that will carry her, and her heart, into untold adventures.

It's with the boys that she has to be careful. She has to take care because their hearts are fragile. The way her father's heart was fragile, the way some things can get broken without anyone even noticing, until it's too late. The boys, still trying to grow into their frames, awkward as giraffes, come to her, palms open; the universal gesture of meaning no harm. All they want is to sit with her, walk with her, lie with her in the grass, fully-clothed, looking into her eyes, watching her face shift between smiling and serious, seeing her father in every expression she lets them have.

To escape it, she would have to move in circles she has no heart to, give her time and her self to the kind of boys who would've beat her father up at school. The kind of boys who would undress her to score points. She has had her fill of these kinds of boys. The freedom gleaned from them not caring whose face she had, was far outstripped by them not caring if her body liked what was being done to it. Before them, she had assumed all things were equal. That her pleasure was as important as theirs. Allowing herself to be reduced to simply a body taught her that a body is not a person, a body is a collection of parts, some of more interest than others. She learned that a person is more than, but cannot exist without, a face, a body, a self.

She has been in love once. It was completely unrequited, by her own willing. She needed it to be. For her, it was a way of testing boundaries. She threw herself at it, safe in the knowledge she would always bounce back untouched. He was a friend of her father's. Desperate to fulfil some kind of unwritten covenant, he had taken her to the basement studio where he and her father hung out, grew up, slept and dreamed. He played the records her father had loved. Together they mouthed the words. Then, on a soft, low couch she fell asleep, her head resting in the warm space beneath his clavicle. His arm folded over her like they were both starlings, and she imagined she was being kept safe under his wing. In half-sleep, she felt the

31

weight of his arm and knew what it was to be loved. Knew that it would have been like that nestling into her father's body.

No boy her own age has elicited in her that same heavy-warm feeling. But it's enough for her that she knows the feeling, would recognise it if it came along.

Some of the boys have come close. The extra-awkward ones, the ones that stammer their dreams quietly into her hair. The ones that only know how to speak through mix-tapes, too unsure of their own voices, of their own abilities to conjure the right words. She keeps a small space in her heart for each of these boys. Like a collector of precious creatures, she thinks this will save them from extinction.

The other girls would wipe them out. But she makes them promise to give these boys safe passage. They see it as kind-heartedness, marvel at the slow, delicate way she has with them, coaxing them out from under their shyness and uncut hair. They watch in wonder, National Geographic-curious, as she teaches these boys to slow dance, gives them names. And every now and then, one boy will dance longer, will hold her in a way she'd forgotten was possible. This boy will get to stay around, to curl into her in sleep, breathe warm on the back of her neck as the stars glow bright above. And when she wakes with the soft of his jeans against her skin, the cotton of his t-shirt brushing her spine, she will let the warmth of it sing in her a little while. She will let herself imagine the possibilities. It will only be as the day wears on, gets its teeth into her, that she will become aware of her face again.

Not every boy will stare. The majority have manners that keep it at an almost-under-the-radar level. She will notice this, and be grateful, despite the familiar tug of disappointment. She will try to distract them with stories and jokes, or with her hands, which she will use to speak for her, when she can't get the words out quick enough. She will flutter them like birds, trying to pull their eyes away from her own, which become like cornflowers left in the rain too long when she doesn't succeed.

The night she spent with her father's friend was one of the first times she realised her power didn't all come from her father. That she was as much her own person, even to those who knew him well, knew him completely. It made her hopeful that it wouldn't always be the same story. That there might be twists and turns she couldn't see coming.

Her father's friends saw a shade of her father, maybe her laugh caught them off guard, or in the dark of a corridor her shape made them stop in their tracks, but as for her face, they tended not to look, or to purposefully look away. And she knew he was there then, in her, and that it hurt his friends to see the one they'd lost. But they didn't leave her. They seemed to sense what it was she needed, offering fragments of old happenings, telling tales of which her father was the star. They tried to bring him alive for her, the father she never knew, and that they knew too well. And she watched them all, tried to find him in the slant of their bodies, in their easy talk and tired eyes, but each time, they had grown a little older, wiser, and in doing so had left her father behind. Ever young. Ever smart-but-not-confident. Ever figuring out who he was, who he was going to be.

As the friends of her father become the men they were meant to be, she is drawn even more to the boys, the boys that are nearly extinct. She finds them everywhere. In all manner of places. In fairy-lit bars; at the Library, beneath piles of French poetry and American prose; under railway arches while trains clatter above; on the street where she lives.

They want to slip their fingers into her hair, brush it away from her face. They want to sit and stand and talk and look. They are full of sadness that her father is dead. This is something that she shares with them. Everywhere, everyone is sad that her father is dead, and it is something she will never be able to not think about. That they see him in her is the thing that kills. But it's okay. Because these boys she's been collecting, these boys with their sad eyes and big ideas, the boys who hold her close when they dance, without it being about anything other than breathing, and being there. These are the boys that give her a glimpse of who her father was. She sees him in all their faces. And reflected back at her, seeing through their eyes, she can at last see herself.

Samson

The story starts here, at the ending of everything. I miss your scent. I miss standing with you in the hallway while you shook off your day. I slept through all of the earthquakes except that first one. The one in the living room, where the walls swayed back and forth and we sat in our chairs and looked across at each other, wide-eyed, stunned into silence. And nothing fell down. Not the way people say happens, anyway. I think the wall between us came loose a little, because from then on, you called me by a different name. And you started bringing me gifts, handing me a new thing you'd made from Lego every time you saw me. First was a house, tiny, not big enough for windows or shutter pieces, just four red oblongs and a white triangle roof. I put it on my bookcase next to the dictionary, so it would be the first thing I always saw. I thought I loved you then. I thought you might be my best friend in the whole world.

The light fitting swung and dizzied us. After the quake, we stood up and sheltered in the doorway, remembering something from films and newsreels. We waited for the aftershock. You were wearing your red woollen jumper with the tear in the cuff. You smelled of forests and bike rides. I don't remember what I was wearing. But I'd had ice cream on the way over. I could feel the sticky of syrup on my thumb and tried to lick it off. You laughed at me then. And we felt close for the first time.

I miss how your arms would reach out wide to tell stories, how words never seemed enough for you. I'd watch your hands as they cut through the air. They were aeroplanes and javelins all at once. They were zip-lines and mountaintops.

The second Lego gift you brought me was a tree. Not the conical one that comes as a standalone piece. This tree you'd made yourself. The trunk was made from three brown squares, and for the leaves you'd used light green and dark green bricks, some fours, some twos, a six and an eight. It was a masterpiece in pixels. I loved it. You didn't talk much that visit. You sat in the corner mostly, quiet while all the other people filled the room with chatter. I couldn't thank you the way I would have liked to. I kept it to words. We hadn't hugged yet, back then. We still had that distance keeping us in our own spaces. I didn't know then how soft the hair was at the back of your neck, or how your skin tasted of salt and moss. I barely knew you at all.

The aftershock came. It was a disappointment. Nothing really moved. We sat in the doorframe playing I Spy, a game that in the confines of a stairwell becomes ridiculous very quickly. After 'carpet' and 'wood' and 'door' and 'stairs', we stretched to 'ceiling' and 'wall' until we had to begin disassembling one another. Hair - eyes - nose - face - lips - mouth - shoulder. Neck - arm - hand - fingers. Everything became so obvious. S could have been shirt or skirt or smile. It was skirt. And T could have been trousers or toe or teeth. It was tongue. But everything we needed was there, on our bodies, or part of our bodies. We made one another aware of different parts of ourselves. With eyes and words and thinking. That you thought of my tongue made me giddy, but I hid it. I stared at your lips but told you my word was leg. And all the while the house stayed standing. But we waited.

I think this is going to be the last time. Everything is so different now. Your father and my mother didn't last. I don't think we ever thought they would. I don't really have a reason to come back here anymore. All my things are packed up. You've been gone for years.

I still have that last Lego piece you gave me. You built me a rocket, red and grey. Not from one of the sets. You never followed the instructions, preferring to make things up as you went along. All the things you gave to me were squared at the edges, and I loved you for that. You were my brother and my friend and everything else. And for the longest time, you kept things together, even while the house was shaking, even after the walls came down.

Lichtenberg

The branches of it spread down across his back. At first I think it's a tattoo, but as I look more closely, I see that it's made up of scar tissue, the skin discoloured a reddish brown. But it's such a beautiful pattern. I take a step closer to get a better look but the guy pulls his shirt down and smoothes it against his body, hiding whatever it was. His friend protests, likes the attention they're getting with this little Show and Tell. I think they're from Accounts. I missed the start of the story. They have amassed a small animated crowd. The party is otherwise muted. The friend lets it go and starts telling a joke. The little crowd listen attentively. He draws them away from the scar guy. I hear laughter but I can't tell if it's fake.

It's not really a party. Someone is leaving. Janet, from payroll. I don't know her. But there are bowls of peanuts and crisps, and a cake with her name on it. It means we don't have to do any work for the next hour, so everyone attends. The guy with the scar turns around and catches me staring. He lowers his head and scans the desk next to him, locates his drink and takes a sip, eyes still down. The carpet tiles here are the scratchy synthetic kind that create so much friction when walking that I have grown accustomed to getting electric shocks. Sometimes I will remember to flatten my hands on my desk, the wood of it, before I leave the office, but mostly I forget, and then I get that jolt as I touch the metal handle to get out.

I don't know that many people here. Everyone tends to stick to their own sections. I spend eight hours a day sitting in a room with Julie and Christine. We know each other's lives inside out. I know Julie will spend one day out of every month sobbing in the bathroom, ochre smears announcing another failure, another 28 days wasted. And I know she can name every single bird native to the British Isles, can recognise each song and tell from a flurry of feathers glimpsed through a closed window if it's a wren or a chaffinch or a lesser spotted kittiwake. And I know Christine spends her nights swallowed in books, her head full of formulas and angles and things to the power of ten. This is not the type of job anyone aspires to. It is a placeholder, until the real job we want comes along. People rarely stay long enough to forge ties outside of their immediate circle. But there are people I will nod to in the hallways, or in meetings. Those I will share smiles with as we dance between the kettle and sink, poorly-timed breaks coinciding, and the over-politeness that follows. Each deferring to the other, neither wanting to seem pushy by accepting. The small awkward rituals of the day to day.

The guy with the scar looks up, finally. I smile and try to look apologetic. I feel bad for staring. He smiles back and takes another sip of his drink. It's not even alcoholic. We're only allowed fizzy grape juice, like we're at some oversized kids' party.

'Sorry about that,' he says. I shake my head. 'He gets overexcited.' He nods towards his friend, who is waving his arms and laughing on the far side of the room.

'Yeah,' I say, 'I figured as much.'

'I'm Dan.' He extends his arm and I move closer to shake his hand.

'Rachel. Nice to meet you.' His handshake is firm, and not clammy. I look at his hand and back up at his face. We let go, but I think we've already held on a fraction too long by then. He has eyes that are nearly black. When he catches my glance he looks away, briefly, then turns

43

back and holds my gaze. 'What is it? The pattern?' I blurt it out. He shapes his mouth to say something and then stops. He holds his hand to his back.

'It's a scar.'

'It's beautiful. What's it from? How--'

'I was struck by lightning.' My face becomes the same as the people's from earlier, a mixture of Oh and Wow and Does It Hurt. He lifts his shirt for me and points to a large central patch of scar tissue. 'This is where the lightning hit. And then it spreads out.'

I reach my fingers out instinctively. 'Can I touch?' He nods. Slowly, I trace the paths the electricity made across Dan's body. The skin is soft, the scar is shallow and thin, branching out like a tree across his whole back. I follow the patterns, my fingertips moving lightly over each line. As Dan breathes, the shapes shift beneath my fingers. I forget where I am. And then I remember. I'm completely, inappropriately in Dan's personal space. He has his eyes closed, but as I right myself and lift my fingers from his skin, he opens them again.

'Hi,' I say, 'sor-ry.'

'No. It's...it's fine.'

'I think I probably owe you a drink after that. Grape juice yeah? On the rocks?' He laughs and manages to

44

dissipate all the awkward. I take his paper cup and head to the cake table and pour refills for us both. When I get back, he's sitting on the desk. He slides a stack of papers out of the way so I can sit beside him. Our elbows bang, and we smile and rearrange our limbs, but we don't inch any further away.

'How long have you worked here?' he asks.

'Just over a year. You?'

'About eight months.'

'Too long!'

'Yep.' He holds his cup with both hands. 'I've never seen you before.'

'Ah, I keep myself well hidden away in the office. I only venture out for crisps and grape juice.'

'Not enough people leave, obviously. To think we could've known each other all this time.' He takes a huge gulp when he says this, then looks down at the floor. It feels like we're joking around, but he makes me think about us being friends, being in each other's lives. He makes me wonder how things would be if we had known each other right from the start. I watch his hands again, the way he fiddles with his cup, unfurls the paper rim on one side then bites at it. And I think about how my hands had been on his skin, under his shirt, across his back. The knots of his spine and the just-above hip place, where his flesh was soft and rounded. Next to me, he breathes in deep and takes another gulp. And I think about how his hands would feel on me, brushing against my skin, tracing lines across my back.

'Dan! Dan, hey man, show Russ your lightning scar.' His friend ambles back over to us and I hear Dan sigh, long and weary.

'This is Neil. He works at the desk next to mine. Neil, Rachel.' We shake hands. I let go straight away.

'Come on, show him your scar.'

Dan presses his lips together and gets to his feet. Silently, he turns his back to Neil and Russ and lifts his shirt, resting his other hand on the desk. He stares forward and breathes slow and hard. His body is all tension. I watch him block out everything. I move my hand across the table and rest it on top of his. He looks down at me and I can't read him, but he doesn't move his hand away.

'Okay,' Dan says and pulls his shirt back down. He turns and sits back down with me. Neil and Russ talk at us for a few minutes, but they quickly realise we are not going to engage with them, so they leave us alone again.

'You okay?'

'I wish I'd never told him.'

'He's just jealous.'

'I know. So, anyway, do you want to do this again sometime?'

'Sure. I think Derek's leaving next week,' I joke, wishful. He laughs, and we swap emails while everyone filters back to their offices.

Later, when it's time to go home, I go to put my hands on my desk, and then I don't. Smiling, I reach for the door.

Acknowledgements

Thank you to my fellow Time Travel Opportunists
Richard Birkin and Nathan Good, and to
Catherine Rogers, Aimee Wilkinson, Ray Robinson,
Mike Wilson, Calum Kerr, Jo Bell, Jonathan Taylor,
Dan Carpenter, Nici West, Jenn Ashworth,
Sian Cummins, Adelle Stripe, Melissa Mann, Mel Carlisle
and all the other writers, editors, publishers and curators
who have encouraged me to tell my stories in print and
out loud, and to Matthew Pegg, for letting me tell
them here.

'Bee' was first published in Jawbreakers.

Mantle Lane Press is a subsidiary of Mantle Arts.
Mantle Arts receives financial support from Arts Council
England and North West Leicestershire District Council.